YARA Shahidi

by Emily Hudd

CAPSTONE PRESS
a capstone imprint

Bright Idea Books are published by Capstone Press
1710 Roe Crest Drive, North Mankato, Minnesota 56003
www.mycapstone.com

Library of Congress Cataloging-in-Publication Data
Names: Hudd, Emily, author.
Title: Yara Shahidi / by Emily Hudd.
Description: North Mankato, MN : Capstone Press, [2020] | Series: Influential people | Includes index.
Identifiers: LCCN 2018058410 (print) | LCCN 2019010349 (ebook) | ISBN 9781543571509 (ebook) | ISBN 9781543571400 (hardcover)
Subjects: LCSH: Shahidi, Yara--Juvenile literature. | Actors--United States--Biography--Juvenile literature.
Classification: LCC PN2287.S357 (ebook) | LCC PN2287.S357 H83 2020 (print) | DDC 791.4502/8092 [B] --dc23
LC record available at https://lccn.loc.gov/2018058410

Editorial Credits
Editor: Claire Vanden Branden
Designer: Becky Daum
Production Specialist: Melissa Martin

Photo Credits
Alamy: Entertainment Pictures, 12–13, Walik Goshorn/MediaPunch Inc, 20–21; AP Images: Richard Shotwell/Invision, cover; Newscom: Byron Purvis/AdMedia, 11; Rex Features: Molly Riley/AP, 18; Shutterstock Images: eanstudio, 30–31, Ga Fullner, 8, Joe Seer, 24, Kathy Hutchins, 6–7, 17, 28, lev radin, 23, Sam Aronov, 14–15, Tinseltown, 5, 26–27

Design Elements: Shutterstock Images

Printed in the United States 5831

TABLE OF CONTENTS

CHAPTER 1

STUDENT AND Actress

Yara Shahidi finished her homework. But her work was not done. Next she began practicing her **lines**. Shahidi is a college student. She is also a famous actress.

Shahidi goes to Harvard University. She started in the fall of 2018. She plans to **major** in social studies. She also wants to major in African American studies. Shahidi is a hard worker. She loves her job. But school always comes first.

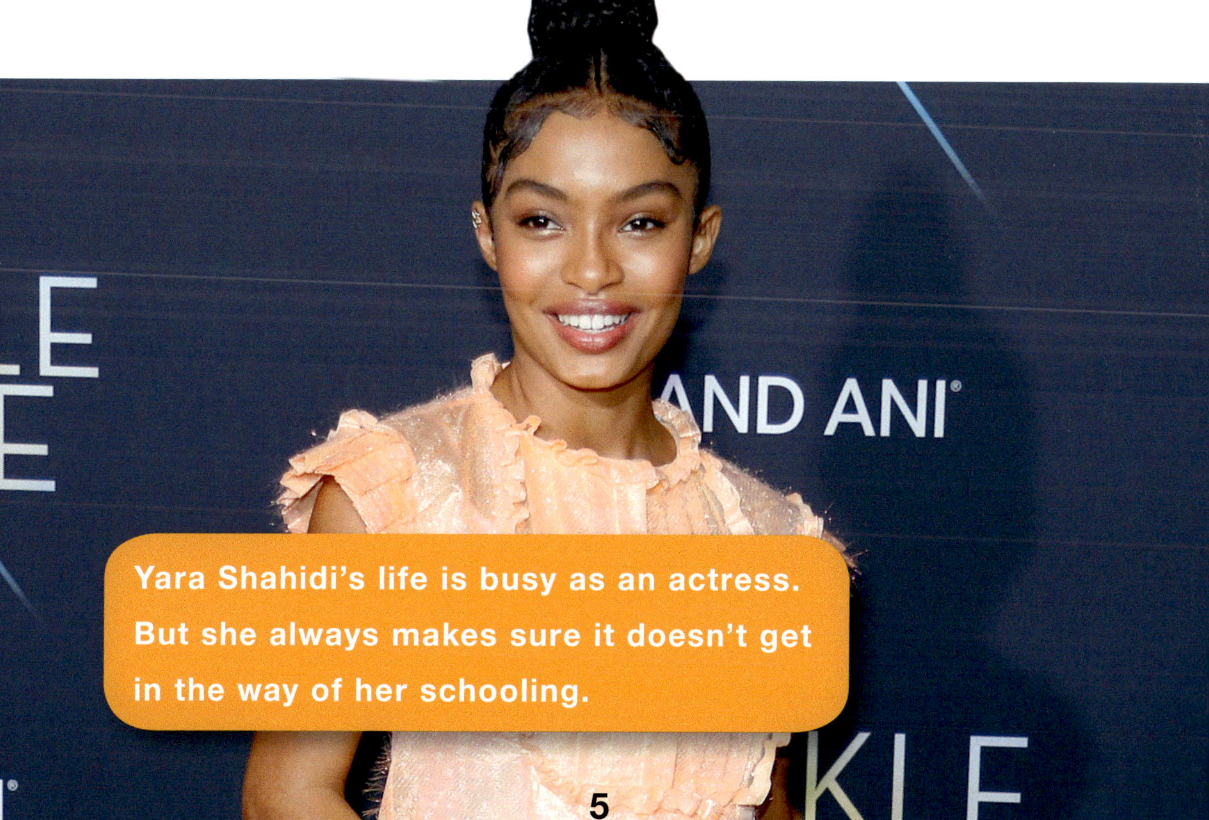

Yara Shahidi's life is busy as an actress. But she always makes sure it doesn't get in the way of her schooling.

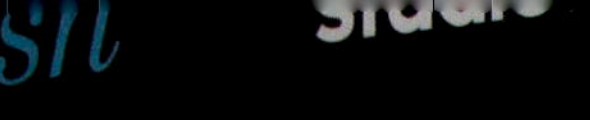

Shahidi (left) with her *Black-ish* co-stars. The show has won many awards.

ACTING

Shahidi acts in a TV show called *Black-ish*. It began in 2014. It is about a black family living in America. Shahidi plays a teenager named Zoey. She was only 14 years old when the show started.

In 2018 Shahidi went on to star in *Grown-ish.* It is based on *Black-ish*. Zoey is still on both shows. Her character goes to college in *Grown-ish*. She learns how to live on her own. Both shows are very popular.

Shahidi is going to college at the same time as her character Zoey. She faces the same problems as Zoey in real life.

CHAPTER 2

EARLY Life

Shahidi was born February 10, 2000. She is from Minneapolis, Minnesota. Shahidi's mother is African American. Her father is Iranian American. Her family later moved to California.

Shahidi has brought her younger brother, Sayeed, to events with her.

Shahidi began acting when she was 6 years old. She was in many different commercials. She learned that she loved to act.

Shahidi starred in *Imagine That* alongside Eddie Murphy.

In 2009 Shahidi landed a big part. She acted in *Imagine That*. It was her first movie. She played a young girl named Olivia.

Shahidi is very close with her parents and her two brothers.

FAMILY MATTERS

Shahidi's parents helped her learn to be confident. They taught her to try her best. They celebrated when she did well in school or acting.

Family is important to Shahidi. She grew up learning about her parents' **cultures**. Shahidi tells people to be proud of their family backgrounds.

CHAPTER 3

HELPING Others

Shahidi cares about helping others. She raises **awareness** for many different causes. Standing up for people of color is important to Shahidi.

Shahidi believes companies need to show more **diversity**. Ads and magazine covers appear in many places. People see them all over the world. Shahidi believes people of all skin colors need to be shown. She wants everyone to feel **represented**.

Shahidi attends events celebrating black artists in Hollywood.

Shahidi (right) and Michelle Obama worked together to help more girls around the world get a good education.

Another important cause to Shahidi is education. In 2016 she teamed up with First Lady Michelle Obama. They worked on Let Girls Learn. It focused on the importance of educating girls.

Shahidi has been awarded for her work for women's rights.

SOCIAL MEDIA

Shahidi talks a lot about women's rights. She tells girls to dream big. She believes women can do anything.

Shahidi uses **social media** to talk about her beliefs. People see her pictures. They watch her videos. People learn about many causes through Shahidi.

MANY FOLLOWERS

Shahidi has more than 3 million followers on Instagram. She has more than 350,000 followers on Twitter.

CHAPTER 4

ALL ABOUT Voting

Shahidi learned about **politics** in school. Leaders make important decisions. They can change laws. Laws can change the way people live. Shahidi wants to help. She wants to make life better for all.

In 2017 Shahidi was named one of the "Most Influential Teens" in *Time* magazine.

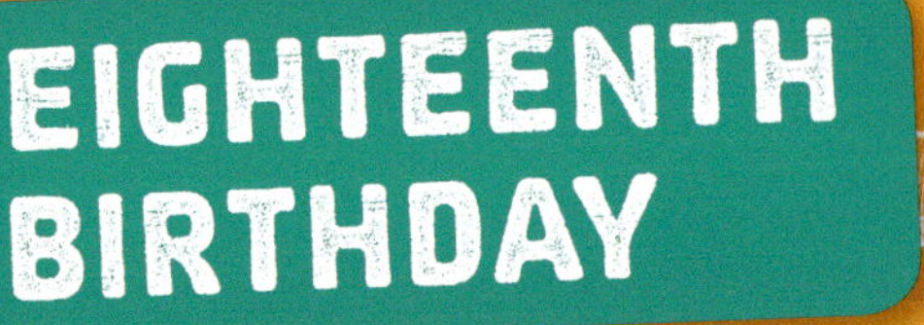

EIGHTEENTH BIRTHDAY

Shahidi was excited to turn 18. She had a special birthday party. People could **register** to vote at her party.

Shahidi created Eighteen x 18 to help teens understand tough issues in politics.

People need to vote to elect leaders. People must be 18 years or older to vote in the United States. But many people don't. Shahidi wants to change that. She wants to get more people to vote.

Shahidi started Eighteen x 18 in 2018. It tells young people why they should vote. It makes voting easier for others.

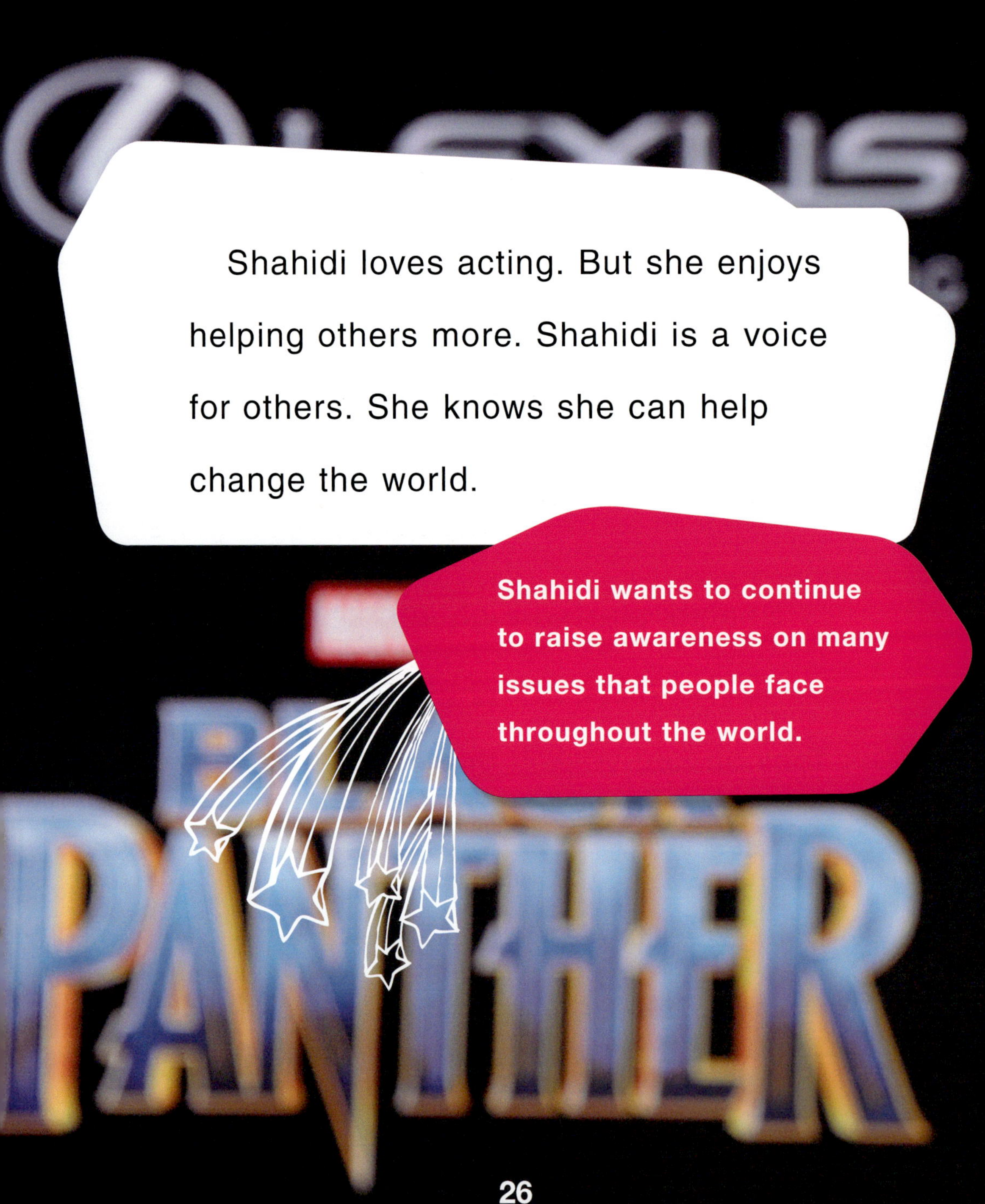

Shahidi loves acting. But she enjoys helping others more. Shahidi is a voice for others. She knows she can help change the world.

Shahidi wants to continue to raise awareness on many issues that people face throughout the world.

GLOSSARY

awareness
having knowledge of something

culture
how a group of people lives, including traditions or beliefs

diversity
the condition of being varied

lines
the words that someone says when they are acting

major
the main subject studied at college

politics
a subject that is about a country and its laws and leaders

register
to sign up

represent
to show what is important to another person or group of people

social media
a form of communication online where people can share ideas, photos, or videos

TIMELINE

2000: Yara Shahidi is born in Minneapolis, Minnesota.

2009: Shahidi acts in her first movie, *Imagine That*.

2014: Shahidi starts acting in *Black-ish*.

2018: Shahidi begins Eighteen x 18 on social media.

2018: Shahidi starts acting in *Grown-ish* as the main character.

2018: Shahidi begins college at Harvard University.

RAISE AWARENESS

Yara Shahidi uses her social media to tell others about important issues. Now it's time for you to raise awareness for a cause that's important to you! Think of a problem that has affected you or someone you know. Then think of ways to help make that problem better. Perhaps someone at your school can't afford lunch. Or maybe an older neighbor has trouble shoveling his sidewalk when it snows. You could come up with an idea to start a fundraiser to help students who need lunch money. Or you could start a group that helps older people in your neighborhood.

Come up with two or three solutions for your problem. Make a 30-second video about the issue. Be sure to speak clearly. Make sure you explain the problem and explain ways for others to get involved. Make it fun and interesting!

FURTHER RESOURCES

Want to make a difference in your community? Learn more with these books:

Clinton, Chelsea. *Start Now: You Can Make a Difference.* New York: Philomel Books, 2018.

Thompson, Laurie Ann. *Be a Changemaker: How to Start Something That Matters.* New York: Simon Pulse, 2014.

Ready to learn about politics? Check out these resources:

DK Find Out!: What Does a Politician Do?
https://www.dkfindout.com/us/more-find-out/what-does-politician-do

Roosevelt, Eleanor, and Michelle Markel. *When You Grow Up to Vote: How Our Government Works for You.* New York: Roaring Brook Press, 2018.

INDEX